Mervyn's Revenge

Clearly nobody *really* cared about him. That much was obvious.

He didn't come down during the packing, and he certainly didn't come down when they all lined up under his tree to say their pitiful goodbyes.

'Look, he's just licking his paw as if we're not here,' said Mrs Freedman sadly.

'Sort of spoils things, doesn't it?' said Sarah.

Now *that* was the best news Mervyn had heard for some time.

'Are you sure he'll be all right?' Tom asked his parents anxiously.

All in all it was a sorry sight, which was just fine by Mervyn. There was no need to help send them off all happy and jolly, winging their way to sand, surf and fresh prawns in the food bowl.

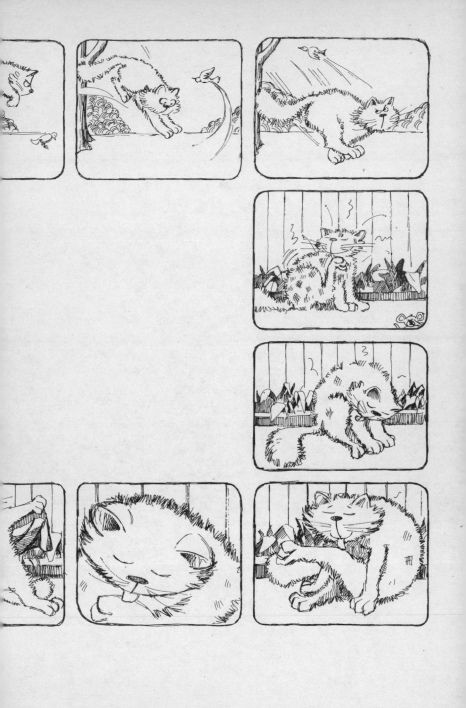

Mervyn's Revenge

Leone Peguero

Illustrated by Shirley Peters

RED FOX

A Red Fox Book

Published by Random House Children's Books
20 Vauxhall Bridge Road, London SW1V 2SA

A division of Random House UK Ltd
London Melbourne Sydney Auckland
Johannesburg and agencies throughout the world

First published in Australia by
Margaret Hamilton Books Pty Ltd 1991

First published in Great Britain by
The Bodley Head Children's Books 1991

Red Fox edition 1992
Reprinted 1992, 1993

Printed and bound in Great Britain by
Cox & Wyman Ltd, Reading, Berks

ISBN 0 09 997520 3

Contents

1 A tasty beginning

Mervyn's morning had been a success.
And that was the opinion of a very fussy
cat.

For starters, there had been a delicious
breakfast of fish fingers. Just the thing to
find in his best food bowl. Mervyn licked
his furry lips at the memory and just in
case there were a few crumbs left.

It seemed that he had finally got the
message through to the Freedman family
that tinned muck was definitely *out*. This
had been a bit of a battle, but at last they'd
begun to realise that he was not the type
for canned cat food. Only properly

prepared meals were welcome on *his*
menu. The rattle of a mere can and opener
failed to excite him.

Tit-bits passed on by the children under
the meal table when the adults weren't
looking, were also fine.

Just this morning, Mervyn had enjoyed
a generous helping of Sarah's sausage and
bacon. 'Afters' had been a handful of
Choco Crunchies from Tom's cereal bowl.

The best thing about these extras was
licking Tom and Sarah's fingers with a
sandpaper tongue, which made them
giggle so much that it was almost as much
fun as the food itself.

It certainly had been a satisfying start
to a promising kind of day.

Later that morning, Mervyn woke from
a refreshing snooze. He decided that a
chance to bother Amos, the little terrier

2

who lived next door with old Elsie
Lavender, was just what was needed to
brighten up the rest of the morning.

He set off slowly along the high fence
between the Freedman's garden and their
neighbour Elsie's. And, as always, this
sent the little wire-haired mutt into bursts
of excited barking, as he tried yet again to
catch Mervyn.

'An old one, but a good one,' reflected
Mervyn, as he completed his stretch along
the boards.

Yes, the morning had been just fine. It
was in the afternoon that things took a
nasty turn for the worse.

2 High-flying news

As midday neared, and the summer sun
warmed overhead, Mervyn decided that
the shady ferns by the side fence would be
the coolest spot to wait for lunch.

His move there took him within earshot
of a conversation between Mrs Freedman
and Elsie Lavender.

Mervyn was not a cat to find the chatter
of humans especially interesting, but this
time a few words caught his ear. 'Holiday',
'very soon' and 'special', told him he should
pay greater attention.

'We are rather looking forward to this
holiday,' Mrs Freedman was saying. 'It's

not our usual spot. And, of course, it will
mean flying.'

'Oooh, flying . . .' Elsie bit her lip
doubtfully. 'Personally, luv, I don't fancy it
m'self.' Then she added quickly with a
smile, never one to dwell on the dismal,
'But, of course it's up to you.'

'Flying!' mused Mervyn. 'Silly woman . . .
Flying's just the thing.' He could already
see himself boarding a jet plane on the set
day. No doubt it would be to some sunny
faraway island.

'It's about time we went somewhere
special,' Mervyn's thoughts ran on. As a
brave cat traveller, he relished the
thought. He turned back to the fencetop
chat, hoping to learn more.

'Don't you worry, dearie,' Elsie was

saying. 'Amos and I will take good care of him. Go right ahead and enjoy yourselves, I say.'

This gave Mervyn something to think about. Who was this poor unfortunate who needed the care of Elsie and her yapping companion? It seemed that one of the family was to miss out on this exciting trip to tropical paradise.

Who could be so unlucky?

3 A nasty shock

Could the unlucky person be Mr
Freedman? Maybe he wasn't able to get
time off work. Was Elsic going to help him
out with a few meals? Mervyn felt sad just
at the thought.

On the other hand, was it Tom? Did he
have school exams he needed to study for?
If so, it wouldn't be the same without him.

Elsie had spoken of 'him', so it couldn't
be Mrs Freedman or Sarah. Mervyn tuned
back in for further clues.

'It would be a shame,' sighed Mrs
Freedman, 'to have to place him in a
cattery. I'm sure he wouldn't like it there.'

Cattery! Mervyn's furry ears flickered wildly at the word and all it suggested. Could this be true?

Surely it was not *he*, Mervyn, who was expected to miss out on tropical paradise! He, who had never missed a holiday yet.

Mervyn was devastated!

The treachery of it all. How *could* they do this to him? The friends to whom he had given the best of his kitten-days. Had they forgotten the warmth and pleasure of a fur-filled lap? And what about all the fun he had shared with them both at home and on holiday? Could this be his reward?

When it really counted, when the chips were down, what did he get? A *cattery*. A cat prison. That's what he got.

While *they* basked on golden sands and

gazed out at clear blue water, he would
spend lonely nights and days in a cat
prison.

It was all very well for Mrs Freedman to
babble on, 'The airlines aren't keen on
pets, and of course the hotels are no
better. Not like our usual holiday spot.
Shame, isn't it?'

'Indeed it is, dear,' agreed Elsie readily.
'Don't stop to think, most of them, do
they?'

Of course, he, Mervyn, would never have
considered for a moment going without
them. But did they mind leaving him?

Apparently not!

'Now, you mustn't be thinking of those cat homes, dearie!' continued kind-hearted Elsie. 'They're all very well, but you know Amos and I will be here. You can count on us. He won't be too much of a bother. We'll take good care of him.'

So the matter was settled, it seemed to Mervyn, as easily as the scoffing of a lightly warmed fish finger.

4 A farewell plan

Over the next few days, Mervyn watched
the family packing excitedly. But he
watched from the top branch of his special
garden tree.

'Here, Mervyn,' he heard Tom shout
anxiously over and over again as, like the
others, he tried to get him to come down.
Then Tom would go and ask anyone who
would listen, 'Why won't he come down?'

'You'd think he knows,' replied Mr
Freedman one time. 'No doubt about those
cats, they seem to know when they're in
for the push.'

The push! The *push*? That word struck

Mervyn like the smell of rotten fish.

'Don't you worry about him,' Elsie comforted them from her side of the fence. 'He'll come down when he's hungry. And Amos and I will be here when he does.'

'Quite right,' agreed Mervyn for once. A few clawfuls of Amos would hardly make up for paradise lost, but at least it would be something to look forward to.

It was quite plain to Mervyn that any worried words being thrown around meant nothing. His family's actions were speaking louder than any words ever could. Clearly nobody *really* cared about him. That much was obvious.

He didn't come down during the packing, and he certainly didn't come down when they all lined up under his tree to say their pitiful goodbyes.

'Look, he's just licking his paw as if we're not here,' said Mrs Freedman sadly.

'Sort of spoils things, doesn't it?' said Sarah.

Now *that* was the best news Mervyn had heard for some time.

'Are you sure he'll be all right?' Tom asked his parents anxiously.

All in all it was a sorry sight, which was just fine by Mervyn. There was no need to help send them off all happy and jolly, winging their way to sand, surf and fresh prawns in the food bowl.

Once the taxi had pulled away, bursting at the seams with the family and their holiday gear, Mervyn sat down for a hard think. That was one goodbye well over and done with. Now it was time to plan his own.

He could, of course, simply swallow his pride and wait patiently for them all to

return. He could sit eagerly by the door each day, and then leap into their arms as soon as they returned.

The very idea disgusted him!

A far better plan came to mind. He could wipe the dust of this home he had known from kitten-days off his paws and leave right now.

This second plan held more appeal. But something, it seemed, was still missing. What could it be?

It wasn't long before Mervyn realised what it was. Yes, it was the bitter-sweet taste of *revenge*.

He would leave in his own good time, but before he did, there was much to be done. He would make everyone realise how he felt at being so shabbily left out of a much-needed holiday.

In short, he would *take his revenge*.

5 Mervyn the trickster

Mervyn's thoughts were interrupted by a loud 'Cooee'. It was Elsie. She was coming along the side passage to the back garden.

She spoke to Mervyn in her usual cheerful voice as soon as she saw him. 'I know you're a bit upset, what with being left behind and all, so I've brought a few special bits and pieces for you to eat.'

Mervyn sat in his tree looking out over the neighbourhood as if no one had spoken.

But Elsie went on as if nothing was wrong. 'I know you're not too pleased with life at the moment, but don't forget, duckie, that Amos and I are just next door and you're not alone.'

Big deal! Mervyn flicked his whiskers crossly. 'Duckie', really!

After Elsie had left, Mervyn bounded down and scoffed up the special tit-bits that she had brought. He then curled up on a garden seat to lay plans.

Mervyn had a store of best-ever tricks that he could pull out of his furry sleeve at short notice. One of his very best was needed right now. He thought back over some of his sure winners.

His gardening game was an old favourite. He would wait until someone, such as Mrs Freedman, was happily weeding the garden, thinking about nothing in particular.

Then when the victim least expected it, he would dive-bomb, right on the weed they were tugging at. Result: hysterical shrieks and a very satisfying fuss.

There was also the one of quickly eating something off the table or kitchen bench, and then lying in an uninterested and sleepy way just to one side. It was excellent fun listening to the others argue over who had taken it.

Scratching hopefully at a window or door to be let in, was another speciality. Someone would at last decide that the cat-flap was locked (of course it wasn't) and get up reluctantly to let him in.

And of course there was always sitting at the top of a tree looking worried and sad. This one was best performed when a kitten. Without fail, some foolish human would risk life and limb trying to get him down.

Then, just as they were losing their grip, Mervyn would float down, as if it was hard to see what all the fuss was about.

18

The trouble with these tricks, Mervyn
knew, was that they had all been done
before. Always worth a replay when one
was at a loss, but this time something new
and daring was needed.

Just the thing turned up that morning
when Elsie came in after shopping with a
brown-paper bag, from which she took a
new plant.

'Aren't you a sweet little thing,'
muttered Elsie to her plant, as she knelt
heavily on the ground and began digging a
home for it in one of her garden beds.

Mervyn saw his chance. Amos was
sound asleep in his kitchen basket, so it
was safe to jump lightly into the yard
and begin the fun.

He set himself
behind the now empty
bag and waited for Elsie to look up. As she
did, Mervyn began to move the bag
towards her by pushing gently against it
with his head and body.

From where Elsie knelt the result was,
of course, rather extraordinary. What she
saw was a paper bag apparently moving
towards her of its own accord.

'Lord, love a duck,' said Elsie
prayerfully. 'What's this now?' she then
added in stronger tones, as it continued to
move towards her.

Elsie was made of sterner stuff than to
turn turtle from a mere paper bag – even
one that could walk. She was also a firm
believer that the Lord helped those who
helped themselves. So with little further
ado she rose and dealt the advancing bag a
fair kick in its middle.

There was a great crackling of paper,
followed by a hideous 'meeooow'.

'Dear me!' Elsie exclaimed in distress, as

Mervyn was revealed in all his
naughtiness. 'It's you, is it?'

Mervyn sprang for the fence and the
safety of his own tree.

'You fair gave me an awful start,' said
Elsie looking up at him. 'I couldn't see one
whisker of you behind that bag, otherwise
I wouldn't have kicked it so.'

Mervyn scrunched up in a hurt,
wounded-looking little ball on a branch of
his tree. This, of course,
only worried Elsie
more.

'I haven't hurt you, have I?' she asked,
all concern for him, having forgotten her
own shock.

'Not hurt me!' muttered Mervyn to
himself. 'Put a foot that size briskly up
your nose, and see if it hurts.'

Mervyn crept further up his tree to lick
his wounds as best he could. Clearly his
plan for revenge had taken a bit of a
set-back. But that, hopefully, would only
be temporary.

6 Mervyn the hunter

There can be no doubt about it. If cats were bigger, human owners would soon be on the Extinct List. That is to say, the hunter instinct is still well and truly alive in the average pussy cat. And Mervyn was no exception.

The thrill of the chase. The joy of surprise. The pleasure of the *kill*! These were all Mervyn's. And when *revenge* is in the air, the hunter's heart takes on new daring.

There she was. Elsie the quarry. The *prey*.

By keeping to shadows, slinking beneath

branches and clumps of leaves, and
lurking behind pot plants, Mervyn was
able to keep up a careful and measured
pace behind Elsie, as she tidied up next
morning in her front garden.

It was a simple, but effective plan. With
Amos cut off behind a half-way fence, it
was also a safe one.

Better still, the postman was on his way.
Mervyn leapt lightly from behind a large
daisy bush to an overhanging tree on the
front fence near the letterbox.

Here was his chance to capture both Elsie and Mick, the postman, with one foul spring – well, at least to give them a bit of a fright!

Just before the planned attack point – the letterbox – Mick leant up against the fence for a chat with Elsie.

'How's the cat doing?'

'Poor luv's not himself, really.'

'Trouble settling down, eh?'

'He'll be all right.'

'What's 'is game, there?' At this point Mick leant his head in Mervyn's direction.

Elsie replied with a twitter, 'Thinks he's a jungle cat, probably. Been following me around like that all morning, poor luv.'

Mick roared with delight at this news, and Elsie joined in with a hearty laugh.

Mervyn, the butt of their laughter, was shocked. He backed off into his own yard for a good sulk. Laugh at him, would they? *He'd show them.*

Mervyn thought briefly of the fish in the bowl in Elsie's living room. Then he decided against them as he didn't fancy getting his paws wet.

Butterflies and mice were also a bit of a speciality for him, but then of course, not always out and about.

No. It would have to be the birds in the tall tree in Elsie's backyard. It was always possible to make a dash up that tree during one of Amos's sleepy moments.

And that was exactly what Mervyn put on his *revenge* plan for the afternoon.

High in the topmost branches he waited patiently for his moment. A de-feathered, blood-stained little body on her front doorstep would soon let Elsie know he meant business.

Just as the whole thing was set up, and every fibre of Mervyn's being was stretched on his task, a howl of dismay shattered the peaceful afternoon.

'Aaaahhh!' screeched Elsie, as she saw what Mervyn was up to.

In turn, Mervyn's fur stood on end and he very nearly lost his footing, while the little bird being stalked fluttered away unharmed.

AAAHHH

'You're a naughty boy, you are!' followed up Elsie unnecessarily. 'Get down from there at once.'

By this time, Amos had been alerted and began to bark wildly in support, so that every bird in the neighbourhood was put on full red alert.

Mervyn padded home in disgust, as Elsie held tightly on to Amos.

'Don't let me see you being so naughty again,' called Elsie, and she went indoors to open a can of chicken and liver, hoping to take his mind off innocent birdies in her backyard.

Once again, *revenge* would have to wait!

7 Mervyn the wrecker . . . is here!

Mervyn was down, but not out! Some
battles might have been lost, but the war
was not over. *Revenge* would still find a
way.

When it came to stirring up trouble,
messy trouble, Mervyn was a master of the
art.

His family took care to keep his efforts
in check, but Mervyn still found a way to
practise his skills. Take graffiti, for
example. Some of his best work had been
completed on rainy days. Most often the
cry would go up, 'Ohh, errr! The cat's wet!'

'Pooh, he smells.'

'Get him away from me.'

Such selfish, thoughtless talk usually meant that he, Mervyn, was turfed outside and the cat-flap locked.

But not to worry. Much, he had learnt, could be made of that. Outside were glorious mud puddles just waiting like an artist's palette.

What next? Well, now it was time to find the best surface for a work of art.

Mervyn's first choice was usually the family car. Sitting there, gleaming, it was a worthy canvas for a true artist.

And there was always the outdoor furniture and painted window sills.

When he was finished and eager to come inside again it was time to work the *guilt* tactic on the family. This was done by choosing a spot outside where they could see him from the warmth and comfort of the sitting room.

By looking truly cold, wet and sad, at

last someone would relent and start the chorus. 'Poor old Mervyn.'

And the others would join in.

'Just look at the poor old thing, will you.'

'It's not fair.'

'He'll catch pneumonia.'

'Oh, all right, let him in again. But keep him away from me.'

This was his chance to sidle back in and finish off what mud was left on his smudgy paw pads. Shining floors, sparkling white microwave cabinets, and velvet chairs, were all excellent for this.

Now that Mervyn's family was away on holiday in tropical paradise, special arrangements had been made. While he could still get inside through the cat-flap, this was only as far as the laundry and his cat basket. The door into the rest of the house was kept closed.

Each day Elsie opened the front door with a key the family had left her, dropped off any letters and junk mail, and checked to make sure everything was in order throughout the house.

One day Mervyn's chance came. Not only did Elsie forget to close the door leading into the house, but it was also a wet and nasty day. Just the day, in fact, for any self-respecting cat to get himself into a warm and comfortable house and make merry.

Once in, Mervyn started to exercise all his skills as a 'home improver'. He hadn't had a decent claw sharpen-up for some time, and the carpeted staircase was just great for that.

The baskets of dried flowers were always good for a quick nibble, until someone caught him. Now that no one was there to shoo him away, he was able to make quite a meal of them.

Neatly arranged jars on shelves were also a challenge. Especially the small jars for spices. Mervyn took a leisurely stroll around the kitchen, taking care *not* to be his usual careful, light-stepping self.

Curtains were always a fun way to have a bit of a scratch and a swing. The fact that any small table nearby might topple

as he whirled by was only to be expected.

When the rain had cleared and he had finished his performance, Mervyn settled down in his tree and waited for the applause.

'Eeeerrrkk!'

That was Elsie on her late-afternoon rounds. A most satisfying sound.

After she had worked her way through a long and careful clean-up, Elsie had a few well-chosen words for Mervyn's ears.

But Mervyn wasn't listening. After all, *revenge* is *sweet*.

8 Mervyn the night prowler

Despite his recent success, the long holiday
break was weighing heavily on Mervyn's
paws. No doubt for the family it was
flying, but back at the cat bowl it was
definitely dragging.

To make the next few days bearable,
some further devilry was called for.
Mervyn knew at once that it should be his
night capers.

If he really threw himself into it, he felt
sure it could be his greatest triumph. After
all, this was no time to hang back. He had
the motive, and the means. Now all that
was needed was the opportunity. And just

such a dark and windy night soon
presented itself.

It was the perfect occasion. There are, of
course, nothing like swirling gusts of wind
to make humans edgy and ready to be
frightened by the special night-prowling
routine Mervyn had in mind.

Elsie and Amos would get the full
treatment!

To set things rolling, he padded softly to
Elsie's bedroom window and gave it a bit of
a bump. Rattles in the night were great to
set teeth chattering.

The next step was to knock over
something like a pot plant, watering can
or, best of all, a rubbish bin.

This evening Mervyn was lucky. He found a lovely rattly tin dustbin and, best of all, managed to set the lid rolling down a slight dip in the path.

'Excellent!' he said to himself.

Now he was ready for the Roof Walk. Luckily, Elsie's roof was made of shiny tin. This meant that his footsteps would sound more like an elephant's than a dainty-footed cat's.

Mervyn got things going with a little old-fashioned cha-cha. Then about mid-roof he tried out one or two new dance steps. After a rousing high leap with half-twist, he finished off nicely with several pirouettes.

This evening he felt certain any judge who knew his stuff would have awarded a score of ten out of ten.

Now for his 'yeowl'.

Mervyn was justifiably proud of his yeowl. He had worked on it long and hard until it could tear strong men and women's nerves to shreds and set their knees knocking.

It worked. Amos was at the window barking loudly. Any time now it would all begin.

Yes, success. The pooch across the street began yapping as well. Then, sure enough, the mutt up the road joined the chorus line. With any luck, the neighbourhood would soon be jumping.

Now it was Elsie's turn. The window was thrust open and a head popped out. 'Who's there?' she called anxiously.

That was when Mervyn, unfortunately, gave the game away. His leap from the roof on to the fence was obvious even in the night gloom.

'Is it you again?' cried Elsie crossly. 'You've been a cross to bear, and that's for certain. We'll have words in the morning, make no mistake.'

'Words,' scoffed Mervyn. The only words Elsie need trouble herself with should be to that heartless family of his when they returned. They were the only ones he hoped would hear all about his dreadful and dastardly deeds of *revenge*.

9 Mervyn the actor

Mervyn couldn't be sure, but he had his
suspicions. It seemed to him that the
Freedman family should be home soon.

Sure enough, Elsie said, 'Won't be long
now, dearie,' bright and early next
morning. Ever forgiving, she failed to
remind him of his night adventures.
Instead she oozed with sympathy.

This was just what Mervyn needed to
play upon. Here was a last-ditch chance to
really get across to *everyone*, the stress,
the misery, of being cruelly left behind.

Mervyn set off on his 'I really couldn't
eat a thing' routine. He tiptoed in an

uninterested way around his food bowl as
Elsie scooped in his breakfast.

'Not feeling too bright?' she cooed, as
Mervyn failed to brush up against her legs
eagerly.

'This is more like it,' thought Mervyn. 'I
should have pulled this one sooner. Could
have had her on the phone telling them to
come home because I'm pining away.'

Mervyn knew to push this one before it
was too late. His whiskers drooped and his
head hung.

'Never mind, luv. You'll probably be
wanting it later,' said Elsie confidently.

'What would *she* know,' thought Mervyn
crossly, as Elsie tottered off to her own
yard. Mervyn could see now that this
would take some working on. He would

have to spend the rest of the morning
thinking his way into his new role as a
   poor
      neglected
        unloved
          sick . . .
            little pussy cat.
To be honest, Mervyn had never really
had a great deal of success with this one
before.

Mrs Freedman was probably the softest
touch, but the other hard-hearts, led by
her husband, were always talking her
down. On it would go.

'Perhaps he's sick.'

'Ha! Fat chance. Bloated, more likely.'

'Perhaps he doesn't like this type of
food.'

'Well he can't be *too* hungry.'

'I'll fix something else.'

'Forget it! We'll see how he feels about it
when he's *really* hungry.'

Mervyn held hopes of a better response
from Elsie. When he saw her coming later
that afternoon, he stirred himself and
wriggled into what he hoped was a long,
thin-looking version of himself. And he put
on a sad, woebegone expression he had
been practising.

Sure enough, *bingo*!

'Well now, you're still not looking so well,' said Elsie as she filled his bowl with fresh food.

She tapped his bowl encouragingly. But Mervyn merely pulled himself to his feet, walked in a sad little circle, and then flopped down again in much the same spot, as if exhausted.

Foolishly, Mervyn had come too close in an effort to achieve the best effect, so that Elsie was able to reach over and touch his nose with her pudgy little fingers. Too late, Mervyn moved out of arm's reach.

'A nice wet, cold little nose you have there, luv. Not too much wrong with you, eh?' And she waddled off, confident that her job as cat-sitter was still well under control.

Mervyn was disgusted. How far did a cat have to go with these heartless humans? Even Elsie refused to take his illness seriously.

Mervyn was so disgusted he couldn't even muster enough energy to stir up Amos with a walk along the fence. Things had certainly come to a sorry state!

10 The homecoming

'Today's the day,' said Elsie to Mervyn the next morning with what sounded like a sigh of relief. 'That family of yours will be back around midday.'

She also mumbled something else as she left that sounded like, 'Can't say I'll be sorry.' But that wasn't the sort of thing Elsie would say. Besides, Mervyn didn't have time to worry. He had other matters to consider.

Soon he would be on centre stage again. How to play it was the thing that concerned him.

Much depended on Elsie and how she

reported his efforts at showing his family just what he thought of them. That is, had his policy for *revenge* worked?

There is, after all, no point in taking your revenge unless your target knows that he or she has had their just desserts.

That Mervyn had been wronged was certain. At least to Mervyn. Now his family must learn of the depth of his injured feelings. He hung close to the fenceline so that he would be at hand when they arrived home and heard the news.

At last a taxi drew up and out jumped Mervyn's family. Elsie heard them too, and met them as they piled out.

'How was your holiday?' she asked
excitedly, and they all chorused back their
own version of 'excellent', much to
Mervyn's disgust.

'Gosh, it seems funny to be home,' said
Tom.

'No more sun and surf,' said his father
wistfully.

'Or breakfast in bed,' said his mother
with a sigh.

'But it's good to come home, too,' said
Sarah, though not very convincingly.

'Where's Mervyn?' asked Tom, looking
about.

'He's around somewhere,' replied Elsie.
'No doubt he'll be here when he realises
you're back, and with such fine suntans,'
she added.

'And how did he fare with us away?' asked Mrs Freedman, as they moved to the front porch.

'Not too bad,' said Elsie good-naturedly. 'We had our silly moments, but nothing to mention.'

Nothing to mention! Mervyn could hardly believe his furry ears. That silly woman! Was there no hate, no anger in her old bones? Couldn't she be trusted to report fully on all of his dastardly deeds in depth and detail?

This was the limit! Mervyn slunk away down the side passage to his tree in the backyard.

'There he goes,' said Tom eagerly, and a general rush followed down the passageway after him.

But Mervyn was too quick. Not only did he manage to climb his tree, but also to drop over the back fence on to a neighbour's shed top, where he knew he could hide out without being seen.

Leave him at home, would they! Return from a trip to tropical paradise and expect everything to go on as before! It just wasn't on. With all else failed, Mervyn had only the pleasure of his company, or rather the *lack* of it, to drive home his feelings to his family.

Having been given the slip, Mervyn's family took themselves inside to unpack. And it was odd just how quickly everything returned to its normal ebb and flow. The only thing that was soon out of the ordinary was that once in a while someone would come into the backyard and call, 'Mervyn, Mervyn.'

'Fat lot of good that will do you,' sniffed Mervyn each time, looking carefully in another direction.

Afternoon turned to night. At the usual time, Amy came out with a meal to place in Mervyn's bowl. Even from where he sat Mervyn could tell what it was. Lightly fried fish fingers! The smell wafted

deliciously up and over his head. She didn't even call him more than once. They were certainly playing a hard game.

But this was the *ultimate revenge*. Mervyn was not about to weaken. Long night turned to morning, and still he knew what must be done. They must pay for their heartlessness. Leaving home was a tough turn to take, but sometimes it was the only way.

Call out as they might before they set out for school, Tom and Sarah could not tempt Mervyn home.

That evening, Mervyn saw Mr Freedman speaking across the fence to Elsie. He edged as close as he dared so that he could tune in.

'Looks like we've lost him for sure,' said
Mr Freedman sadly.

'Surely not,' said Elsie in return.

'The children are really upset.'

Mervyn began to feel quite cheered at
this news.

'So they would be,' agreed Elsie.

'I'm a great believer in animal
replacement,' said Mr Freedman firmly.

'How do y'mean "replacement"?' asked
Elsie with interest.

Mervyn's interest level was also rising.

'Oh, you know. Get a new kitten
straight away. Take the children's mind
off their loss,' said Mr Freedman. 'Perhaps
two kittens,' he added thoughtfully.

Mervyn slunk, or rather staggered in
shock, back to his hiding place. A kitten,
perhaps *two* of them, at *his* cat bowl! The
idea was unthinkable.

Later that evening Mervyn made his decision. 'Yes,' he thought, 'they've had enough.' Obviously they were breaking under the stress of his final plan of revenge.

Staying away had made them think twice. To even be considering the nuisance of a silly little kitten about the place, was a clear indication that something had snapped. That they were thinking of getting *two* kittens, was proof positive.

It was time he let them off the hook of life without him.

Mervyn put his nose high in the air, lifted his furry toes in the haughtiest manner, and marched through a cat-flap thoughtfully left open, and once again back into the Freedman family's life.